KB194297

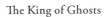

The King of Ghosts

The King of Ghosts

A collection of new poems by Kim An
Translated by Jein Han

귀신의 왕　김안

K-Poet Series 042

ASIA

Contents

THE KING
OF GHOSTS

Mimesis

A monk was walking, his whole body on fire. I was trailing close behind. It was the appetizing smell that made me follow him. Eventually the monk's body burned down and the fire alone continued to walk, trembling with hunger. With no eyes but two giant arms, the famished fire swung its limbs like a raging red monkey. I was seized with the impulse to grab the fire's strange arms. It was the same impulse I felt during last night's dream where I wandered through a golden cornfield and found a dead body that I yearned to embrace. *You poor thing, you starved thing, the vast endless darkness has its eye on you. If you keep your eyes closed, you'll never open them again*, I said, in an attempt to persuade. Persuade whom? The corpse. Mind you, this was a dream. I didn't want us to die. The corpse hesitated, then replied: *I am but a fuzzy story drifting like fog. I am a story that only exists in the dark pocket of night.* A small flame bloomed from the corpse's forehead, turned into a small moth, and bumped into my forehead. I opened my eyes. In front of me, a giant fire was staggering forward. It moved like a cloud performing a slow dance. I took a step forward to walk into the fire. It was at that moment that I remembered the corpse's last words. *Open your eyes and see the real world. A paradise of fire that has frozen to death. Thing's you've experienced but can't explain. Desires.* I embraced the corpse. Like ashes in a brazier, I could feel myself slowly drifting away.

Snowman, the Beginning

Who is it that has gathered my scattered body. Who has called me back to this world of soiled whiteness from the vague darkness darker than black. When I stroke my face, my eyes, nose, and mouth fall off. Should I lead the rest of my life by miming how I imagine the rest of it should go? While I hesitate, birds with their heads on fire fly by and the season when flowers bloom like bewildered gods will soon spread like a wildfire, like anxiety, as that red, white, and yellow liquid surges into my bones, so why would I need to impersonate another man's life. At noon, the shadows of those who resemble me leave the earth and I remain alone as an anomaly. Beside me, a man hangs from a tree. He stretches out his arms and legs to wrap himself around the tree. At first glance he looks like a cicada, but on closer inspection I can tell he has a similar form and composition to me. Dangling from the tree in a position no human being has ever assumed, he uses his shell that is slashed by rain, his crumbling face, and his claws that have disappeared without a trace after being broken, cracked, and worn away, to hold on to the peak of winter. His pitiful struggle resembled my questions about life, but all I could do was melt in front of him into a puddle of dirty water, and think of someone who has lost their face after facing the winter of their life. The man's white blood vessels touched me and began to leak. The story begins.

Poppy

Sitting on the lawn, I raise my head. The winter mountain range was stretching out, dry and flat, like a sickly snake. The birds were tuning the instruments hanging in the air. On one side of the lawn was a small tree that was long dead, and buried under that tree was a puppy. I raised that puppy at the clueless age of six, often feeding it leftover rice and milk. The puppy was brought to keep me company while everyone else was at work but I no longer remember its name. There were other residents in the house where I, who often suffered from stomach aches, and the puppy, who often suffered from hunger, lived. The landlord lived on the second floor, you, Yujin, lived on the first floor, and my family lived in the small subdivided unit. The red brick house had a yard. On one side of the yard was a toilet that no one used and planted next to the toilet was the small tree. Sometimes, when I would squat in the yard alone and bask in the sun, the tree would look like it was walking over to me like a dwarf god. Each time, I would hear the birds that had finished their tuning sing songs that sounded like prerecorded screams, and from the shaman's house that I called *The King of Ghosts* at the end of the alley I would hear the fevered moan of the house's spirit. (Only later did I realized that it wasn't the moan of a spirit but the sound of unethical love.) I assumed these sounds came from the ferocious beasts of snow, and that they would soon melt away. One day, listening to the sound of the beasts, I swallowed the snow piled on the dwarf god's shoulder and fell into a three-day sleep. I woke up to the feeling of something licking me. The wet towel on my forehead slid down. Next to me was my mother, curled up and sound asleep from exhaustion as her round back heaved. She was freezing, white. The tree, also tired, no longer moved.

Yujin

On my way home from work, I was stuck in traffic. It was unusual for this street to be jammed. There aren't that many people who commute from this old, remote area, so I assumed there was an accident blocking up the road. Horns blared from all directions. Up ahead, an old man with a bicycle was jaywalking. His back hunched and face tanned, the old man hung his head low as he stumbled to the middle of the road. *You crazy old bastard, are you trying to kill yourself?* Someone shouted out their window. But the old man continued to drag his bicycle, slowly, as if he couldn't hear anything and had been walking in the same direction for a long distance. In some way, it looked like the bicycle was hauling a dead man. The sound of the broken bicycle chain dragging on the road. The sound of horns. The sound of bicycle wheels rolling. When I was young, I had seen a similar sight. It was when Yujin's father, who lived across our house, died. Everyone lived together in a narrow alleyway, but his face especially eludes me. He had no job and always sat in front of his home, head hung low. He never responded to any of the neighbors, including his own family, as if he was forced into the family. But after he died, the wheels on the rusty bicycle in front of Yujin's house started spinning on their own. When I crouched in fear of the sound, my mother would comfort me that the wheels were turning because Yujin was crying, and that it would stop after a few days. After a few days, the wheels stopped. And after that day, Yujin stopped growing. She hung her head low and dragged her feet, her back hunched like the mound on a small grave. *That's because she's carrying her father on her back. But after she stopped crying, she buried the bicycle in the mountain behind the house*, said the feeble flame that was burning in the seat next to me. Startled, I turned my head and found myself alone in the middle of an empty road at dawn.

Firm Grip

I was thrown out of home for breaking the only mirror in the house. *Oh, who will take pity on me now. Who will pity me now, you rotten bastard. You should've perished in my belly.* Mother buried her head like a headless beast and howled at the shards of the broken mirror. Her cries were so loud that Poppy, secretly buried under a tree on one side of the lawn, woke up and new leaves sprouted from the dead tree like sharp claws. It was so loud that even the pendulum of the broken clock started moving again. I was beaten. I must have been beaten to death. As I fled, Mother threw shards of the mirror at me. They looked like the frightful fangs of winter. *Never come back. If I see you I'll swallow your ankle.* Crying, I escaped the neighborhood. The countless alleys hissed and slithered like snakes. *Where do I go now? Where do I go now? Who will pity me now?* The words forever hovered in my mouth, the words lingered. Mother must still be crying in her windowless room....... When I opened my eyes, I was lying in the windowless room. Mother was stroking my face. The pendulum of the clock was moving. *Mom, Mom, here's the mirror I broke the other day.* I pointed to the round pendulum of the clock. My mother's hands that were caressing my face began to grow like the black roots of a tree. I couldn't run because I had no feet.

Sleep Paralysis

Dawn. I woke up to find the dreams that had accompanied me all night sitting on top of me, whispering. *Is he still asleep? Shh, you're going to wake him.* I pretended to be asleep so I could eavesdrop on their private conversations and write down their words. *That explains why my body has felt numb all over lately, as if a strange village had fallen on me,* I thought. The youngest of the dreams, the one I'd just dreamed, the one that was just born and was yet to grow any arms or mouth, began to thrash its body, perhaps because I was awake. An older dream opened its red mouth and swallowed the younger one. I felt a cold, sharp ball of fire go down my throat. *It was a curious little dream, running wild like a goat. Swallowing young nightmares like this is the way of my people. It's how ghosts are born.* I wondered why all my dreams were sitting on my body like this, and concluded that it must be because before I went to bed last night, I played the music of a guitarist that had committed suicide. He lost all his memories due to an arteriovenous malformation and forgot who he was, what phrases he had written, and even how to play the guitar. He had to relearn the guitar from scratch by listening to his own albums and watching videos of himself playing, and the things sitting on my body seemed to be memories from before the arteriovenous malformation. Somehow, whenever I listened to his music, blurry shadows would roam the house and each time, the old dog huddled in the corner would bare its gums that were redder than blood, staring anxiously in all directions, which I attributed to dementia. When I reached out to calm him down, he bit my hand. *You can't even recognize your owner. I shouldn't have dug you out from under the tree.* But now that I can't move my body, I think the dog was trying to lead me out of the house. Recently, things began to go awry in the house. The pillars warped, cracking the gray concrete and exposing black, rotten snakes instead of nails. The wind would push the walls inward, turning the house into a single room, and occasionally the pane of glass would billow and bulge. When I poked the window, I would hear a shattering sound but the glass would get even more taut. I blamed it all on my drunkenness, but that wasn't the case. I was devastated. *But at least I have the mirror. This house and this mirror are all I've inherited.* In front of this mirror, my father, myself, and my son would get dressed up to go out. But for some time the fog in the mirror wouldn't clear. That was probably when it all started. Of course, every day I would drunkenly wipe off the fog inside the mirror. That was my daily routine. Sometimes, when I squinted like my drunken father used to do, I could see a figure. It was either a man crouching over a dead dog, or a dog crying on top of a dead man.

Deathday

Late November afternoon, I was sitting at the kitchen table in a daze. The fact that the phone hadn't rung yet meant I'd be sitting here until tomorrow. I let out a heavy sigh. A long shadow appeared, reaching all the way to the ceiling. It was my mother. She asked me if I was eating well and opened the refrigerator door. I was surprised and pleased to see her after such a long time, like a puppy full of curiosity. "Mom, what was the name of the puppy I had when I was a child?" *What puppy?* "I feel like that puppy, seeing you after such a long time." The refrigerator was emitting mist and a white, cool light. Leaving the refrigerator door open,

Mother came over and patted my head. *We never had a puppy.* "No, we had a puppy back when I was six or seven and we lived in the alleyway with the shaman's house. It starved or was beaten to death, so Father buried it under a tree by the bathroom," I replied, biting Mother's fresh wrist like a hungry animal. Mother lovingly offered me her wrist and stroked my hair with her other hand. *You don't have a father.* Come to think of it, I had no memory of him. Why didn't I know that? When I was a child, black shadows slipped in through the window at night and wrapped around my mother's body, did I consider the shadows as my father? My mother gave me her other wrist. *It was the alley, my child.* With both arms gone, she slithered like a snake into the refrigerator, which was white, deep, cool, and silent. The red shadows that spilled out of her arms stretched out like an alley at night.

The King of Ghosts

I tossed a pile of books into my bag. I had to finish the research paper I'd been working on for months. When I stepped out of the house, it was snowing heavily. When did it started snowing? The sky was clear when I was inside the house. The snow was ankle-deep, white, and blinding. I squinted and walked carefully until I reached the bus stop. An old woman was sitting there. The ground under her feet was yellow and frozen, emitting a terrible odor. The snow didn't stop, the bus didn't come, and the light and stench distracted me, so I went back home. The next day I went out again. It was snowing heavily. The bus stop seemed further away than yesterday. I blamed the weather. When I got to the bus stop, the ground was yellow and frozen, and the stench was still there. The bus never came. I walked back home. Over the next few days, the bus stop got farther and farther away, until yesterday morning when it was on the corner of the alley's entrance. I guess today it's going to be inside the alley. If the bus arrives at all. I threw another pile of books into my bag and left the house. It didn't snow today. I walked under white sunshine. I made a turn at the alley where the bus stop had been moved. Inside the alley was the bus stop and the old woman I had seen a few days ago was hunched over. She was plucking and eating grass roots with a broken knife, but she looked a little younger. She looked at me with a smile and said, "I am the alleyway." I couldn't understand what she was saying, so I just stared at her. She was getting younger and younger, and the alley with the bus stop had turned into an unfamiliar landscape. "I am the alleyway." The sun was shining, but it started to snow inside the alley. When I was chased away, the people who lived in the alley began to feel the pang of hunger. Along with hunger, they began to mix desire with impulses. Snow was falling on the branches. The sound of branches weighing down with snow and springing up again. The sound of clean snow blanketing the dirty snow. "I am the alleyway. It feels strange to be here again." I, too, was overcome by a strange feeling and realized that I could not move. The alley, submerged in my memory, stretched out its limbs and grabbed me. Perhaps it had been expanding its dark flesh ever so slowly. Yes, this alley is where my life took place. My mouth spoke words I couldn't understand. "I am the alley you spoke of, I am speaking to you now and I am dead." The old woman's eyes had become dark, deep caves. A cave of rumbling sounds and blue light. A cave that grew larger and larger, closing in on me.

My mind followed the silent breath of the cave and began to run away from my body, running around in a frenzy, like a puppy jumping around with a bell around its neck. I knew the name of that puppy.

Hearing Loss

I woke up to find my ears were gone.
I put my finger in the hole where my ear used
    to be, and it seemed to suck in my finger.
Look, my ears are gone,
I said to my sleeping wife, but there was no
    reply.
I lifted the pillow and blanket, but could not
    find them.

Are you done looking?
I looked everywhere but couldn't find them.
Try straining your ears and listen for a strange
    sound. That's where they probably are.
Listen, I can't hear without my ears.

Disappointed, I went to the living room and sat
at the dining table. They have to somewhere
in the house.

I could hear the chair slowly eroding.

I got up and looked under the chair, but all I
saw was a cloud of dust drifting like a soft
white dream.

Are you done looking?

I couldn't find the ears in the living room, the
bedroom, or the kitchen.

I looked out the window as the day arrived
slowly.

Try straining your ears, no matter how far they

are, your ears will hear something.
I told you I don't have my ears.

I heard something knocking on the window.
    Looking closer, I saw it was the ghost of the
    night.
It had been knocking on the window until
    daybreak. Which was why I had sixty-four
    dreams last night.
When I opened the window
the ghost of the night yawned and rubbed its
    eyes
as it made its way into the bedroom as dark as a
    mud puddle.

Are you done looking? Have you searched both
    inside and out?

Look, are you taunting me?

Angry, I followed the ghost into the bedroom.

Fumbling across the muddy floor I climbed up
    the bed

and removed my sleeping wife's ears and
    attached them to my head.

When morning came, the sickly ghost glared at
    me from inside the picture of my dead wife.

It was the sixty-fifth dream.

Neighbor

It has been raining heavily for days. I lie in my room and think of the names of all the things that float on water. Buds, paper, wooden chopsticks, pens, clothes, hair, pupils, rotten tree roots, hearts. Sometimes I hear a siren outside my window. The cars must be jammed in the pouring rain. The children still go to school despite the downpour. My neighbor's children leave their home noisily. One of them had one leg and bragged that he had four fathers. This happened three years ago, and I have yet to meet any of those fathers. Last holiday, a few of my neighbor's guests rang my doorbell by mistake, but they all looked too old to be the child's father. They all had thin, cloudy eyes, and didn't seem surprised to see me open the door. Some of them tried to come into my house. Some of them are still in my house. They seem to roam the house only when I'm asleep or stare at me from behind. One, two, three. My neighbor had four children, and the third and fourth were twins. The child with one leg was one of the twins. But I hadn't seen him in a while. Probably because I don't leave the house. One, two, three. For days during the downpour, I would lie in my room and listen to my neighbors' children going to and from school, counting and listening to their footsteps.

I couldn't hear the footsteps of the child with one leg. Today is no different. When the rain stops, I should go out when the children leave for school. I toss and turn, trying to figure out how to discreetly ask the neighbor about the child with one leg. Sometimes the strangers in my house try to wake me. Hey, I'm already awake. I've never been asleep. But they keep yelling in an incoherent language. I cover my ears and curl up into a ball. In fact, I always lie down, regardless of the rain. I have to find a way to fall asleep. When I uncover my ears, it is night and my ear is stuck to the wall facing my neighbor's house. So this is why it was noisy every night. When I stand up to remove my ear from the wall, the sound amplifies. I hear a huge roar of water coming from next door. A family struggling to make ends meet has committed suicide by burning a coal briquette in a closed room. Fire trucks have been called to put out the fire. It has been raining heavily for days, and I still haven't floated to the surface.

Red Spider Lilly

More celebrated for his literary talent than his
    life, he
used to teach me that people failed to
    distinguish
humility from actual incompetence. Otherwise,
he said, you'd be treated like a blind librarian
or a mute opera singer.

I didn't write down all of his words
but wrote what existed between his lines—
winter's white fingertip running down my spine,
water boiling in giant cauldron and the sound
    of children's hearts slowly simmering and
    hardening—

so I faced him whenever he called me.

Whenever he pointed out that the conjunctions
    in my sentences were like rusty screws
the chair I was sitting on creaked.
When he said my sentences were like a sutra
    read through broken glasses
his hands, numerous as fibrous roots, covered
    my head but

one day, when he, suffering from rumours and
    no one to meet,
called me, I saw him standing among the spider
    lilies,

his hair raised. That moment, my head turned
   around.
I had no choice but walk backwards toward him
   and when he saw me,
his head fell to the ground, and I could no
   longer distinguish him from the spider lilies.

Ash and Fish

He always painted things that were hunted.
They looked so alive, as if they would pounce
on you the moment you opened the door. *Still
alive?* I was gripping the doorknob. Things
that were so vividly dying. Things that would
spread a smell, like the wind seeping through
a solid wall. He slapped his brush so hard on
the canvas that the easel shook, then looked
at me and said it was just a painting, that they
were neither alive nor dead, so I should open
the door. His eyes were like transparent silver-
gray fish. I grabbed the doorknob and told him
I didn't want to open the door, that I thought
the beings in the paintings would come in if I

did. He stood up and put his hand, the color of silver poplar tree bark covered in moss, on my shoulder and my hand holding the doorknob. Each time he squeezed my hand, crystalline fish danced. It was a transparent dance that spread across his face. His hands reeked of dance's fishy smell. The smell enveloped me.

*

You are being caressed. You do not know who the hands belonged to, but you were laid down on a wet bed, you don't know who laid you down, or what the memory that laid you down was, or who the captain of the ship called *Life* was that brought you here, or what kind of wood the ship was made of, but someone gave you an injection, and you watched like a bystander as the transparent drug spread through your veins. So who was the owner of the hand? Was it a hand? Was it someone's kicking foot? When you dragged your worn leather bag through the door and tried to get out, or when you spent the night with the stranger for the last time, was it feet that rained down on you? You question your memory. Memories are often opaque, distorting or destroying reality. This memory must be wrong. You are surely lying here, you watch yourself lying down as your body turns to ash, but you cannot recognize the hand or the foot that touched you.

*

When Ernest Hoschedé went bankrupt, Claude Monet and his wife, Camille Doncieux, invited him and his family to their house. Hoschedé soon left the house, but his wife Alice and her children stayed with Monet. Camille Doncieux, who was ill, was tormented by the secret relationship between Monet and Alice, but had no choice but to rely on Alice who looked after the sick Camille. In 1879, Camille died. On that day, Claude Monet painted Camille, his muse, on her death bed. After Camille died, Alice destroyed all of Camille's photographs and the letters she exchanged with Monet. In 1891, when Hoschedé died, Alice married Monet.

Kang Yo-bae*

It was a white and crumpling cold. November lay down on the dry, cold ground. On the odorless ground of November, we held a funeral for those who froze to death. The sunlight was watery and opaque. Dead birds were scattered under the roof. I looked up to see black birds gathered in the trees, falling to the ground one by one. The king of the dead birds was looking down at his broken wings. "We are a yellow flame that continues to blaze," it murmured, like a man standing under the sun for the first time after a long battle with sickness. Friends and mothers of the deceased were beating their chests as they cried. They clung to me, sobbing, but I couldn't hear what they were saying. In the distance stood an old dog, its belly bulging like a snowball. White and round. It wriggled like a mountain beast, pushing the invisible village up the hill like a magic trick. The old dog trod toward the village of his birth, dragging his bulging belly. Someone tugged my hand. Friends and fathers of the deceased were beating their chests as they dug with their bare hands. Crouching among them, I dug the frozen earth. The funeral would never end. Everyone at the funeral wept as they dug the ground together. November's claws cut into everyone's hands, turning the ground a dark red. "The funeral will be over soon," said the king of the dead birds, but I didn't believe him. I stood up, staggering like a wet beast, and looked down at the bent backs spewing white steam. That was when I heard it. The old dog had collapsed at the entrance to the village. Its bloated belly burst open and a long yellow flame was born. November dragged the flame by its hair. The flame became a river of lead that circled our funeral. The old houses, the decapitated statues, sank slowly into the leaden river, like a faint dream of the river watching old, terrible memories. I crossed the river and walked out of the painting. Most of the people in the painting were walking without feet. On my way back from the museum I lost one of my shoes. I fell asleep under a blanket that was longer than the night.

* Kang Yo-bae (b. 1952) is a Korean painter.

Literary Pilgrimage

I did a head count to check if everyone was here. Someone was missing. The bus driver was growing impatient and asked when we were leaving. I checked off every name on the list, and yet someone was still missing. I called out the names again, but nothing changed. A younger professor urged me that it was time to go, so I got on the bus. I don't know how I ended up being the guide of this tour, I don't know who didn't show up, they say we're going to a visit a poet's birthplace, but I don't know his name, and I don't know anything so I just stared out the bus window. Well, I had to do something if I wanted to find my footing here.

Meanwhile, the bus arrived at its destination. A young professor announced that the poet's great-grandfather had specially invited us to spend the night, that there would be a writing contest today, and that he had invited me to be a special judge. The bus driver turned his head to look at me in surprise, and I pretended to stare ahead indifferently. I hadn't heard anything about being a judge, but I was glad to have something to do. I read the poem carved in a stele in front of the house and looked around. A low, tattered gray wall surrounded the poet's house, and white feathers were scattered along the wall. "It must be the work of a cat," I muttered. "Yes, he's a sneaky, cruel old thing." I turned to see a man standing beside me. He seemed to be the caretaker of the place. The tall, red-faced man said it had been a long time since an outsider had visited this place, and it was rewarding to see that there were still people who remembered the poet's poems. I nodded politely and smiled. "I often see my dead wife here on spring nights, and that's the fleeting blessing of spring," he said. Raising his hand in the air, he continued. "Look at that sky." The red clouds were swirling low as they slowly dispersed, like evening's bride. "This is a sign that my wife will visit me tonight." Tiny sparks tumbled across the grass as, and the sky grew redder and redder, staining the snow that had yet to melt. "I'm actually the father of the poet." I turned my head and looked at the man. His clothes were inside out, and behind him, the people who seemed to live in the neighborhood were also claiming to be the poet's father. They were all holding things featured in the poet's work: stones, conch shells, bird heads, dense fog, dark hands clutching tree roots, unpleasant memories, and animal cries. The man dressed inside out said, "As you have found us, we have found you, my son." Startled, I ran from them. As I ran, the tour bus sank to the bottom of the water. Everyone was hunched over, fumbling the dark red floor of the poet's birthplace. One seat was still empty.

Insomnia

I awoke in a familiar bar. Sitting at a long table were the CEO of my former workplace, my former boss, and some of my former colleagues. I couldn't understand why I had been summoned to this unexpected meeting. They were discussing the latest literary trends or how political beliefs should be represented in art. I reached for a cigarette and tried to come to my senses. I realized that I had been struggling with insomnia for days, that I had fallen asleep, and that this gathering was just a dream. I was finally asleep. But the fact that this was my dream was a little disappointing. I lit a cigarette and stared at the familiar and unfamiliar scene and faces my dream created. It's perfect, too perfect. I smiled and lit another cigarette, only to get into a fight with the people at the next table. A group of dark and drunk men overturned the table. Everyone started running away in unison. Chased by the drunks, I tried to remember who they were, but I couldn't. Some of them are still looking for me in my house,, even after waking from the dream, so I have to leave all the lights on in the house, even in the middle of the night. A few days ago, when I forgot that the light was off in the bathroom and opened the door without thinking, I found one of them washing his hair in the sink. The bathroom was all black and white because of the white steam and the dark figure. He looked back at me and nonchalantly brushed back his shiny hair, black as a raven. He told me that we should forgive each other of past mistakes, that what mattered was the here and now. Black water ran down his body, and beneath his dark feet, where the water pooled, I could hear the drunken chatter of the revelers. The voices were familiar, and a puff of cigarette smoke rose up to the black and white landscape.

Karma

Father died. The room I am in is no longer familiar. I wonder what dreams this room will trigger tonight. They say one's absence becomes present. This must mean absence is a space created by sewing together ethics and evasion. On the bed is a blanket longer than the night. There, where my father once lay, his illness lingers, suffering on its own. The illness, gasping for air, is the only familiar thing in the room, so I walk over and lie on top of it.

After a long battle with sickness I am standing under the sun. Like soft white water splashing against hard black stone, November creeps up my armpits and numbs my stomach. White petals murmur as they fall. The other night, an angel had passed by my door and I was afraid I would expose what was most precious to me. That moment, the night stole my breath with its quick hand. For a swift second, strange hot beasts danced inside my body. Like a miracle, I awoke. *It's a miracle*, I murmured.

I wake up the sound of someone flushing the toilet. My family is all asleep. I push the long blanket deeper into the night and go to the bathroom. When I come back, someone is lying in my place. "Who are you and why are you lying in my bed?" I whisper so I don't wake my family, but the man doesn't wake up. Furious,

I pull back the blanket that covers him, but it has no end. *How long is this blanket?* I mutter to myself in amazement as I tug the blanket which was longer than the night. I collapse in exhaustion after pulling and pulling all night.

I opened my eyes to find myself in an unfamiliar room. Who will take pity on me now. I couldn't move. My dark and thick hair grew out, wrapping around my body so I couldn't move. Just as I was wondering who would set me free, someone with no feet came up to me. Crying, they cut my hair. *An angel*, I thought. *The angel must have gotten in because I left the window open. Look, feathers of ice are fluttering.* But I couldn't tell which would be longer, my hair or the night.

The sun had exhausted its white light, exposing its red flesh. I return and lie back down. This is a very traditional method of drowning. I am currently underwater. The neighborhood where I first learned to speak is also underwater. The water piles neatly over my body. It's November. When I open my eyes, I see thin feathers of ice drifting. I have made a room underwater. I am an undrying ghost. As I begin to dream of ghosts, the thing that is most precious to me enters my dreams.

Cicada

It was a clear, cold winter day. I rubbed my frozen hands together as I walked. *How strange, why are there no pockents on my clothes?* I was curious, but figured it was because my wife hadn't come home in four days. Dawn. Winter. There was no one walking or sleeping on the streets, only the occasional car driving at high speed, tearing through the clenched maw of winter, transparent and silent. I was at a crossroads waiting for the light to change when I felt a strange sensation. I rubbed my frozen hands together as I looked around. There was nothing but a black, slender winter tree and the shell of an old cicada. Upon closer inspection,

I realized that the cicada had frozen to death while it was molting. The cicada was trembling its thin wings with all its might. *A summer that has withered, a summer that has frozen.* As a child, I used to tie a cicada to a string and spin it around and around. Each time it would cry louder and louder. *Make the summer end. Make it end,* I chanted. I thought that would end the summer, and I guess it did. But now I had no string, no pockets, no wife. *I am not alive*, the old cicada said. *That's nonsense. Your wings, your belly full of cold white nothingness, your body the color of wood. You look like the other cicadas I have seen, the same cicadas that ended that terrible summer with me*, I replied. *Do you think it is possible to speak to me? Do you believe this certain uncertainty? Then I am not alive*, replied the cicada. The cicada had a point, but I couldn't make sense of the situation. I thought that the cicada was being a bit garrulous and stubborn. I rubbed my frozen hands together and thought for a moment of my wife. *I am not alive. I am not a cicada that always repeats the same sound. I'm a summer that has withered, a summer that has frozen*. As the cicada droned on like a pointless prayer, I began to lose interest. There was no one on the streets, the cars were gone, and even the traffic lights were frozen and out of order. Winter was drawing a thin deep line across my forehead. I rubbed my frozen hands together as I crossed the empty street. *I'm a summer that has withered, a summer that has frozen*, the cicada continued to chirp. I looked back from the other side of the road. From the mountain range spread out like a folding screen behind the winter trees, the sun that had exhausted its chilling white light was exposing the red flesh of evening.

Pedrolino

I am out of work. I am no longer a clown. I do not mean it metaphorically. Clown. The one who makes you laugh. The one who makes faces you've never seen before. The one who studies the use of obvious objects. The one who is older than any story you know. The one who, from a story, pulls out a forest, a desk, wine, a balloon. The one who flies so low that people assume they are a flightless bird. The one who apologizes in advance, disappears in advance, only to return posthumously in a daze. The one who considers themself a dreamer, the one who always spits out words that fail. Metaphors on clowns are so abundant they don't need further explanation, but if, by any chance, you wish to become a clown,

 you must be a worthless child that amounts to nothing, you must be able to sleep in a bag for days on end, you must be able to hear the sound of rats fattening in the dark under the floor, you must be able to wait like a statue praying with broken hands, you must be the head of a martyr silently decaying, the smirk on the face of an informant after mocking a failed revolutionist, you must be able to suffer from a desire that is inexplicable, even though you've experienced it first hand, as your four limbs are tied to a loveless bed that surges, you must regard that hesitation as hope, and like a undrying ghost, you must be able to leave wet footprints even without feet.

This is a story from an ancient rulebook on the profession. The man known as the greatest clown in history grew up without a mirror and used a round clock pendulum instead. Each day, he swung his head in sync with the pendulum, and before he knew it, his head alone was left behind, moving in front of the clock. Under the illustration, it states: "He is dead. There will be no resurrection."* In every edition you read, you'll find this page dog-eared.

  * Youn Kyung Hee (윤경희), *Die Wunderkammer* (『분더카머』), Moon-ji, 2021, p. 243.

壎

It had been a while since we've seen each other. It had been so long that we had nothing to say after asking each other, *How have you been?* After a while, she carefully told me that she was soon going to see her parents. I had never heard her talk about her parents so I asked what they were like. Squinting, she continued to talk as if she were pulling out an old beast trapped in the cave of memory. "We used to pluck grass. We plucked grass until they passed away." She said she was planning to meet her parents, walk with them, and climb the hill where they had used to pluck grass when she was young. She closed her eyes for a moment, then opened them. A bright, round light spread across her face. *Ah*, I briefly exclaimed. I had seen that light before. It was the light that had sparkled in my sister's eyes before she turned into an instrument. "I can still feel the resentment in my fingers. I can't do anything with these hands." Crying day and night, my sister never left her room until she turned into a small instrument the shape of an urn. I couldn't touch it, so I left it in her room. Sometimes, on windy days, the instrument would make a low, muffled sound all by itself, and the ghosts who couldn't leave the village would try to enter the house, clinging to the windows. Tormented by the sound of the instrument that was once my sister and the commotion of the ghosts, I opened the window. That was when the woman had entered the house. *Even angels must be afraid of that place.* I looked at the woman. She was already fading away. I wondered when she would return, but I didn't dare ask. *She'll probably come back a new person*, I muttered to myself.

Mimesis

That winter, it appeared that I had died. Or perhaps I was in a similar state. I carefully uncurled my fingers bent by the harsh winter. When I was young, there had been rumors about a girl found dead in the old factory at the end of the alley that sprawled out like fine roots. The adults had whispered about how her lower body was bruised and covered in blood. The sound of splitting steel I used to hear whenever I walked past the factory echoed from my fingers. The sound was so loud that it awoke the ghosts hiding inside the stones. *Don't go into the forest*, the ghosts used to tell me. They walked by, from village to village, from forest to forest, emitting mist and a dark blue chill. I followed. I knew how this would eventually end, but according to the book my father used to read, the ghosts were composed of unfathomable elements, and though my father was dead his voice lived on in the book. A being that only endures as a voice in a book. I could hear the sound of steel splitting whenever I turned the pages, the sound of the ghosts rushing between my legs. The sound swelled and I surrendered, which was a natural conclusion. I stood before a black stone field. Beyond the stone field, the black forest spewed white smoke like the sweaty back of a wild beast. Winter gashed at the trees with sharp white claws and the trees writhed in pain. It was as if the ghosts, sitting on the stones, were sending me their final warning. Soon they turned into old snakes and coiled their bodies into round rocks. I entered the black forest, carefully walking past the whispering stone field like a feeble priest who had lost faith. Inside the forest was a golden corn field, redder and more radiant than blood. It was as if I was seeing the landscape through another body. My body tried to hold onto the mind. *Don't let go. You'll fall off.* I heard the voice of my body, but that was twenty years ago, and I thought about how difficult it was to overturn my entire mind.

My body screeched like steel and tried to grab onto my mind again, but I covered my ears with my hands. My earholes started to eat my hands. When I wrested off my hands from my ears, long strings of stories spilled out of my ears. It was the voice of a white, watery ghost that would slip through the door crack every night since that day. I followed the voice into the cornfield, thrusting my whole body into the darkness. Old age, red stains, and watery wraiths began to ooze from my ears, serpentine and endless.

POET'S NOTE

POET

My childhood memories concentrate around a single alley. A dead-end, downhill alley that stretched out for about eighty meters. Dilapidated houses lined both sides of the alley's shallow slope, and at the end was a house. Three families lived in the house. The landlord lived in the front room on the second floor, the other two families lived in the front and back rooms on the first floor. I lived in the small room on the back side of the building. There was also a puppy. Unlike others, there was more that I lacked than I had, but it didn't feel like it. Most of the people who lived in the houses lining the alley seemed to know each other well. I still remember some of their names: Sanghoon, Hakbae, Mikyung, and Yujin. There was one house in particular that was closed shut. A house where red and white shaman banners fluttered. I wondered who lived there. Sometimes someone would sit quietly in front of the door and stir gossip, but my younger self had larger questions.

The feeling I got from that the alley, or rather the house, overlapped with stories I used to hear from my mother's side of the family. The story about seeing an imugi, a dragon in a nascent stage, being swept away in a flood. The story about digging up Grandfather's grave when the family was in great distress to find the hair, fingernails, and toenails on his corpse grown twice as long as his height. The story about finding a large serpent coiled on a well and being healed of illness after performing a ceremony for the serpent. These strange stories traveled through my body like a fever and infiltrated my low dreams.

Well over thirty, my family moved back to the

same neighborhood because our livelihood was once again destitute. Unlike others, there was more that we lacked than we had. We had no puppy, no car, no money. There are no names that I remember. But I never felt like I lacked anything. Nothing was mine to begin with. They never belonged to me, as they should be.

Now I am well over forty and far away from that place. I now have things I never had. I have a house, a car, a few books with my name on them, a wife and a daughter. I seem to even have a social title since some call me a teacher and some call me a writer. Of course, there are things that are missing and gone. I don't have a puppy, my father is gone, the workplace I used to go every day is gone. Then or now, I do not feel as if I lack anything. What is gone is gone, and what exists will not last forever. However,

I no longer believe in the stories I overheard from my mother's family or the eeriness that the shuttered house used to make me feel. But I can't say they are non-existent. There are things that cross over from my low dreams. And writing is what lets me experience them.

*

Thus I open the door that leads to what is invisible. I listen to the sound of invisible beings come in and murmur. From afar, they look white and cloudy, like a fish hunched over. I take a step toward them. What unfolds is nothing but an illusion of my own making, but it is still unknown territory to me. Writing is the act of bringing out what my consciousness has erased. Those erased things with strange textures make me, define me, and bind me. Things that have been erased from me. These are things alreadyn recorded by the gods but they are things I have not seen. Non-beings.

I think about the song sung by Shantideva: "When neither beings nor non-beings appear to the mind, the mind is free from entanglement." Shantideva spoke before a crowd that demanded a lecture unlike any they've heard before in order to exile him. As Shantideva spoke, his body slowly disappeared and only his words remained in the air. A state where neither being nor non-being arises in the mind. That is a state of emptiness.

With this beautiful story in front of me, I continue to write. Words become the song of the spirit and emptiness. In front of the Buddhist mantra that true emptiness is the amalgam of various relationships, my writing pales in comparison. I cannot touch the 'mad elephant of the mind,' let alone hold it firmly. Yet I seek to find its origin in my recent writings. The process of choosing my words and rewriting my sentences only confirms my foolishness. This is the fifth time I've written something out of foolishness and presented it to the world to read.

*

Through the act of writing, I am able to reach a state of clarity and dream of a precarious tension between sin and ethics. In Buddhism, human beings are called "manusya," or 'beings that think.' Writing is what confirms thought. But from time to time, it leads me to a state of erasure in which I witness a landscape of commotion. To me, poetry is a sign of that commotion. I write poetry by refining and revising that commotion. And now, the commotion is over.

POET'S ESSAY

I wander in front of beautiful words and beautiful music. I grow old as I wander. They cannot become my own. They are like water, cold and clear, that slips out of my hands. I grow old as I try to hold on to them. I look at the paths of water spreading out from my hand and think. What is the origin of this water?

*

In the beginning there is always a memory. More precisely, there is the mind. Memories are an obsession of the mind. But we should be more precise. There is memory, there is the mind, and there is obsession. Obsession exists because of feelings, feelings exists because of collision and because of you who collided with me. In the beginning there is you. You are shaking. And this is where my thoughts stop due to beauty.

There are stories that you, who are beautiful as you waver, left behind. Of course you had no intention of leaving them behind, but I am still holding on to those stories. Because your body still exists in this story. Your breath, your movements, your life that moves along the path of breath and water. That is what my writing is directed toward. That is probably what I wanted to say in my first book, no matter how much I hate to admit it. Someone will call it Pravritti.

*

In Songhak-dong, Incheon, there is a tunnel called Hongyemun. It was built by the Japanese Army in 1908, and was called "hyeolmun" because it drilled a hole in the mountain. It is a small tunnel on the top of a steep road where only one car can pass at a time. At that time, this tunnel divided the residential area of the Japanese and the Koreans. Recently, I came across an interesting article from 1923 related to the tunnel. On the tunnel's wall, someone wrote "水平社員來仁記念." "水平社" is an organization founded in 1922 to liberate the burakumin, the lowest caste in Japan. Their founding manifesto was the first human rights declaration in Japan, and they interacted with "Hyeongpyeongsa," an organization created in Jinju in 1923 to abolish discrimination against baekjeong.

There has been forms of discrimination and people who wanted to change it. There were those who saw movements in colonial empire and wished it would spread to their colonized homeland. There were rugged hands that scribbled that wish on walls. We must look at those hands through the eyes of the past, not the eyes of the present that already knows the outcome of history. Only then can we see the despair of the people who used to live on this land.

Back then, there were no burakumin living in the Japanese settlements in Korea, so the words on the wall must have been written by a Korean. It must have been a Korean hand. Their country was gone. Their life was dire. Because there was no hope, they must have wanted to hold on to something, anything. They must have heard about the human rights movement happening in the colonial empire, and the hand must have wanted to hold on to that. There must have been a foolish yet desperate hope that the lives of the lowest caste, whether they lived in the empire or the colony, were the same, and that they could unite beyond the barriers of country and nation.

I found that beautiful. The dark hope, the hand that had to hold on to it, and the individual lives that slipped through the hands and history that transcended all. And above all the sadness that even today, this republic stays the same. The scribble on the tunnel's wall read like a cry, a cry that grabbed on to anything and begged for pity. I wanted to translate that cry, and that is what I wanted to convey in my second book. The world that I was in contact with was full of pain. What I felt was what some people call ethics.

*

There is a single picture. It is a picture of my daughter when she was around four years old. The photo is taken from behind and she is riding on my shoulders. In that photo, my shoulders appear wider than they actually are. It is because I am carrying the weight of another being. Some beings refract themselves onto others. The two undergo an existential transformation. It was a time when the two of us felt like we couldn't live without each other. When we wholeheartedly felt what it meant to give up our lives for someone else. When sunlight poured down on my daughter and my back.

We were passing through a beautiful time. It was a time when wounds healed beautifully.

Silence was the only language that could fully convey it. On the other side, there was language. There was the commotion of language. There was the foulness and hypocrisy of those who used language and the evil they committed. As I passed through it all, I was in turmoil. It was as if each day I oscillated between extremes. Those were the days when I oscillated between atonement and light. Days of ignorance and indifference. Days of witness. Days of bankruptcy.

The emotion that haunted me the most was fear. I was afraid my shoulders would melt down and the being I was supposed to hold up would fall. It felt like my happiness was built on someone's firm misery. If I had been a better poet, I would have stepped further into that fear. But I hesitated. I assumed I was already sufficiently afraid. To endure that fear I needed a tautology. I needed a single name. This is a clumsy excuse for my third book that included many poems with the same title. It was borne out of fear, the consciousness of my fear.

*

Twenty years have passed.

After twenty years, some things have disappeared. Things that I wanted to hold on to. Language cannot fully capture the sadness. One person disappeared, and I wandered after becoming similar to that person. I saw twenty-five others who were also similar, and each time I was startled. Each time my face twisted with an unfamiliar feeling that was neither joy, surprise, or sadness. The face I made also resembled that one person. The one person I struggled to not resemble.

After that one person disappeared, many others followed suit. Each time, I seem to become that one face. My body scatters as I become two, then three, and then reunite with the twenty-five others who resemble that one person. Perhaps this is because I do not know how to name that feeling. Even in the secular world I have become many people, met many people, and yet I still do not know the name of that feeling. So I decided to call it 'my entire heart.' My fourth book is about the search for its name, and I have yet to find a name for that feeling.

*

To dance on the edge of the border. On the border of madness and reason. The border of a madman and a philosopher. I believe this is one of the ultimate states of writing. I always tried to write with this in mind. But looking back, my writing, and even this essay, resembles the madness of Yajnadatta. It is said that Yajnadatta was deep in thought as he looked into a mirror. The man in the mirror had a head, but he didn't. He grabbed people and asked if they've seen his head. I believe my writing is similar to his question. Even when I had no material results, I had been writing poetry every day.

And yet I write another book. It is in part because of the request of my favorite writers, but it is also because I wanted to travel upstream and retrace the stream that has made me who I am today.

*

"Leave me alone! Be careful! You're pushing me towards the abyss!

   — You've already fallen into the abyss!"*

* Pascal Quignard, *Rhetorique Speculative* (『파스칼 키냐르의 수사학』), tr. 백선희, Eulyoo Publishing, 2023, p. 135-136.

COMMENTARY

The Poet's Mirror

Jeong Woo-shin (Poet)

You are following someone. You do not know how long you've been walking but when you look around, no one is there. In the dark, you hear sounds you do not usually hear. They sound like whispers. You turn toward the sound and see someone's heel. You call out, but the person doesn't answer. Excited to see another human, you go to tug their sleeve but they disappear. Your feet refuse to move. Was it a ghost? You continue to walk and realize a snake is following you. You see your own desire mirrored in the snake's face. It no longer matters how far you've walked or who you were following. The moment you take an interest in desire, an impersonal power, you are in danger. Desire is not of this world. Desire has already escaped your body and yet you dream of molting. You are unaware that you have swallowed your own body and are looking for traces of yourself. You are not afraid to abandon your limbs and turn to ashes. You recite a ghost tale that states "I was following close behind" ("Mimesis"). You are the one who simultaneously speaks and listens, the one who crosses dimensions to reshape time and space, the one who mixes childhood memories with future events and casts a black net over them, the one who "always repents in advance, disappears

in advance, appears in a posthumous stupor"
("Pedrolio")-a ghost.

The ghost that inhabits Kim An's *The King of Ghosts* owns a myeonggyeong (明鏡). The dictionary defines myeonggyeong first as "clear mirror" and second as "a mirror on the road to the underworld." It is a mirror in the underworld that reflects the good deeds and bad deeds of the deceased. How did the ghost become "an undrying ghost who creates a room underwater" ("Karma") and the King of Ghosts? Why did he stare blankly at the sight of his "Mother burying her head like a headless beast and howling at broken pieces of the mirror" ("Firm Grip")? As you walk through a dark and damp landscape, you begin to hear voices from beyond your discord with the self or the world. Voices asking to be saved, claiming that they are still alive. It is as if objects are speaking to you. The mirror simultaneously reflects "the alleyway where my life happened" ("The King of Ghosts") and "the frantic moans of the spirit of the shaman's house at the end of the alley that was called the King of Ghosts" ("Poppy"). The concrete and the abstract, the human and the inhuman are bound together in the poet's body.

In life, we exchange the energy that is inside us. It is difficult to recognize the origin and end of the energy that exists inside us. We know that it is in motion. We send our energy to our loved ones. Loved ones can give energy back to the poetic "I," but they can also reject it. If so the "I" will seek energy elsewhere. When even that fails, the "I" will eat away at himself. Energy appears to operate alongside our perception and emotions, but that is not always the case.

It is impossible to control, like desire. Ghosts have no physical body to receive energy. A ghost cannot collect anything. When a human feels as if energy no longer circulates in their body, they become ghosts.

In *The King of Ghosts*, one of the best poems that describe the route of a ghost is "Deathday." The first person the ghost encounters is his mother. His mother "asks if I'm eating well and opens the fridge." On the anniversary of her death, Mother visits to check the refrigerator. The speaker is happy to see his mother. When he asks his mother what the name of his childhood puppy was, she seems perplexed. The speaker asks again about the puppy that either starved to death or was beaten to death when he was young, but the mother replies that they never had a dog. At this point, the titular "deathday" refers to that of the puppy. The speaker bites his mother's wrist like a hungry animal and moves on to ask about his father. The mother replies that he doesn't have a father. The puppy's death now evokes memories of Father's death. Toward the end of the poem, the mother's wrist becomes the alleyway, and ends with the red shadows that spilled from her arm extending as long as the alleyway at night. The speaker travels between his mother, puppy, father, and childhood, searching for traces of himself. At this point, the title seems to refer to the anniversary of every family member's death. When the emotions that tied you to a loved one is broken, when nothing in the world belongs to you, the speaker choses the mouth and ears of a ghost. In reality, this is evolution. In fantasy, this is devolution. Or perhaps the opposite. The ghost that appears in this collection jump from poetic object to poetic object, and paves an alley for itself.

The King of Ghosts is both a narrative and a moving image made up of countless frames. Images that are repeated in a single poem cross over into other poems. Sentences slither like a snake and create collisions. They touch the speaker's heart and transform him. Eventually, it becomes impossible to find the original ghost. The first and last poems in the collection, "Mimesis" and "Mimesis," are like two giant full-length mirrors. The two mirrors face each other, and the ghost cannot escape the alleyway. November, winter, water, light, roundness, whiteness, and trees are the ghost's flesh and bone. These pieces of flesh are repeated, from phoneme to phrase to sentence. They expand between the lines, seep in, and are transformed. A world for the living becomes hospitable for ghosts. You can see this in poems like "Snowman, the Beginning," "Yujin," "Sleep Paralysis," "The King of Ghosts," "Neighbor," "Literary Pilgrimage," "Karma," and "Cicada." When the speaker approaches a poetic object to capture it or engage in a conversation, it transforms into something else or disappears as if an illusion. How beautiful. Reading the poems, you may find yourself lost or mesmerized by things you can see but cannot reach. Things you can reach but cannot see. You become anxious. You can only observe the poet's life and perseverance from afar. Your heart aches.

You are still following someone. You wonder if you should just "playact what I assume will

be the rest of my life" ("Snowman, the Beginning").
You abandon your family, your limbs, and
pride. You may become 'Poppy' or 'Yujin,' you
may make faces like the 'Cicada' or the 'Clown.'
You can no longer enter houses in the alley.
You are not welcome anywhere on this earth.
You had no shares to begin with. Because you
are human but also a ghost. How did it come
to this point? Is it because you write literature?
Because the "certain uncertainty" ("Cicada") of
literature destroyed your life? Why do dreams,
(un)consciousness, and madness treat your body
like a playground? You straighten your glasses
and take out the mirror that resembles "winter's
fangs" ("Firm Grip"). To revise your work. To
write your next poem. You offer up everything
you hold dear. Even as you watch "old age,
redness, and dilution wobble" ("Mimesis") as they

reach into your flesh and steal what little that remains, you still contemplate your next poem. What *The King of Ghosts* accomplishes through walking is the 'poet-Pedrolino.' You are the one who, like a clown, creates art by turning your life into an imitation, the one who uses "a round clock pendulum as a mirror" and "studies the use of obvious objects," "the one who is older than any story you know," "the one who, from a story, pulls out a forest, a desk, wine, a balloon," "the one who always spits out words that fail." You are a poet. A ghost. The "undrying ghost" ("Pedrolino") follows the poet.

PRAISES FOR
KIM AN

[Kim An] seeks to put into words the failure that comes with honesty, and what can only be reached through that failure. Therefore, in the midst of our useless and futile "labor of language," we must also desire something that is "one and only." Something unnamable, unspeakable, invisible. And yet something we must struggle to find. Only the form of that fate will sustain us and make the agony bearable. No, that is how it must be. Literature and poets are not forms of institutions but forms of existence and fate that must be practiced.

–Kim Jeonghyun, "To Fail Harder than Anyone Else,"
Lyric Poetry and Poetics, vol. 84, 2019.

[Kim An's] poems do not ask questions that lead to answers that already conform to the social consensus and notions of our time. They criticize the broadest agreements and the process of that consensus, and take us to the forefront of awareness. If life is something that cannot be reverted after crossing the line, after reading Kim An's poems, we will find ourselves in a world of sound darkness, vibrant melancholy, and coherent grief.

— Cho Jae-Ryong, "Questions raised as a Citizen-Poet"
(critical commentary for *Miserere*)

In the third chapter of Vie Secrete, Pascal Quignard suggests that most masterpieces written by humanity disappear into obscurity. He adds that "the absence of these works in humanity's memory must be present as an absence, as a lack. That is my belief." Similarly, in Kim An's poetry, we recognize the human figure through an absence. The most beautiful images of humans are not only not realized but also not testified. They are forgotten in silence. Kim's poems remind us of silence. The silence tells us: when you look back, there is something approaching in the shadow of history. There is a human figure that humans dreamed of.

— Park Dongeok, "A Human Who is Not Historicized,"
Writers, Summer, 2024.

Through images and statements that encompass the social life and trajectory of language, [Kim An] depicts the structures of society and reality, and the human lives that struggle to survive within that structure.

— Judge's commentary for the 19th Hyeondaesi Award

In an era when it is difficult to hold on to our humanity and poetry, [Kim An] confesses that "what I tried to write in my youth was a form of poverty" and "a shameful purgatory / full of excuses and deceit." I was impressed by Kim's continuous attempts at "failing" and "moving forward." I decided to join the poet on his journey toward the future of poetry as his "recitation becomes a silent reading" at his "address written on my last mail," listening to "someone I don't know boiling white noodles and cracking an egg, / someone opening the refrigerator / someone sitting at a round table and facing someone else" (Mazeppa). (…) It is a dark, unpredictable time, and yet writing poetry is like befriending "a foolish ghost who poured out its whole heart" ("Whole Heart") .

    – Judge's commentary for the 3rd Shin Dong-mun Award

K-POET
The King of Ghosts

Written by Kim An
Translated by Jein Han
Published by ASIA Publishers
Address 445, Hoedong-gil, Paju-si, Gyeonggi-do, Korea
(Seoul Office: 161-1, Seodal-ro, Dongjak-gu,Seoul, Korea)
Email bookasia@hanmail.net
ISBN 979-11-5662-317-5 (set) | 979-11-5662-730-2 (04810)
First published in Korea by ASIA Publishers 2024

*This book is published with the support of the Literature Translation Institute of Korea
(LTI Korea).